J. G. Captain Johnston

Which Was Right?

A Story of an International Yacht Race

J. G. Captain Johnston

Which Was Right?
A Story of an International Yacht Race

ISBN/EAN: 9783337404000

Printed in Europe, USA, Canada, Australia, Japan

Cover: Foto ©Andreas Hilbeck / pixelio.de

More available books at **www.hansebooks.com**

WHICH WAS RIGHT?

A STORY OF AN INTERNATIONAL

YACHT RACE. . . . .

BY

CAPTAIN J. G. JOHNSTON,

OF KEY WEST.

WHICH WAS RIGHT?

A STORY OF AN INTERNATIONAL YACHT RACE.

EARLY in the month of November, 1694, great interest was aroused among the American people by the announcement published in the newspapers that an English sportsman had decided to issue a challenge for a contest to decide the ownership of the great international yachting trophy. Details were lacking, but sufficient information had been forthcoming to indicate that a determined effort was to be made by the Englishman to recover the coveted cup. Time and again had attempts been made to win back the emblem, symbolical of supremacy in the sport of yachting, which had been brought to America years before by a boat whose name had been thereafter indissolubly connected with it. Each time the Englishmen had sent over their best boat, manned and captained by their most experienced sailors. Each time they had been met and defeated by a superior boat manned and captained by better sailors. Each defeat had apparently only added to the intensity of the desire to recover their lost prestige, until at the time this latest attempt became known to the public there was not a man, woman or child in the tight little isle who did not consider himself or herself to have a direct personal interest in the success of the enterprise.

It was not at all surprising that this feeling should be duplicated, though obviously inspired by a directly opposite desire as to the outcome, in the people of this country. True, repeated, unqualified success had somewhat dulled the intensity of the popular interest. This was noticeable particularly when the first announcement was made. But when, during the following month of December, details of the challenge were made public, and it was realized that a greater and more determined effort than ever was to be made to take the cup from us, popular feeling was awakened and the subject became the all-absorbing topic of conversation.

This interest was increased somewhat by the fact that at the outset seemingly unsurmountable obstacles appeared to rise up in the path of the diplomatists to whom had been intrusted the arrangement of the details preliminary to the acceptance of the challenge. To prevent the Americans from being taken unawares by a not too scrupulous challenger, there had some years previously been executed a deed of gift of the trophy to the leading yachting organization of this country, by which it was hedged about by stringent and clearly defined conditions. These conditions had not been fully observed in the challenge that had been issued, and a controversy arose, which at one time threatened to end in the breaking off of all negotiations.

Voluminous correspondence passed between the representatives of the persons directly interested in both countries. The newspapers on both sides of the Atlantic took up the discussion, and a decidedly varied, if not absorbing, battle was waged.

Finally, a compromise was reached by concessions being made by both sides, and early in the following year the conditions of the prospective race were agreed upon. The decision was hailed with delight by the public. The people had become wearied by the long drawn out controversy, but now that a race was assured, past differences of opinion were forgotten and contentions forgiven.

There now arose in America the question as to who should build the boat that was destined to meet the Englishman. Previous experience in that connection prompted certain wealthy yachtsmen to keep well in the background during the preliminary discussion of the question, but withal there were hundreds of ambitious sportsmen ready to lend a helping hand and become identified with an enterprise that, judged from the view-point of popularity, promised to be satisfactory, whether crowned by a successful issue or not.

Discretion marked the selection of the organization having the matter in charge, however, and three of the wealthiest and most popular yachtsmen in the country were chosen. There were many who were disappointed naturally, but so well was the choice received by the press and public, that no word of dis-. satisfaction was allowed to extend beyond their immediate circle of friends and sympathizers. Two of the gentlemen selected, as chance would have it, were men of vast business enterprises. The third, as chance would also have it, was a gentleman of leisure. To the latter naturally fell the arduous task of attending to the details of the construction of the boat. As a matter of fact, he was given entire charge of the enterprise, with *carte blanche* as to expenditure.

It was decided at the outset that nothing but the best that this country could produce in the shape of a yacht would meet the requirements of the occasion. To this end the foremost builder of racing yachts was communicated with. Several conferences between the gentlemen composing the syndicate and the builder were held, with the result that it was finally agreed that all details should be left to the builder and the gentleman having the greatest amount of time to devote to them.

Preparations for the construction of the boat were made forthwith and work on it was started at once. The greatest secrecy was observed. No one, with the exception of the builders, the active member of the syndicate and the workmen engaged, was allowed near her. This secrecy, it was announced, was necessary to prevent the exact model of the boat from being made public, thereby giving the English adversary a presumed advantage. To so great an extent was this precaution carried, that different workmen were employed to construct different parts of the boat. Thus it transpired that, when completed, there were only two or three of the vast number of men who had been at work upon the boat who were conversant with all the details of construction.

During the months that elapsed while the boat was being built, little items concerning her were allowed to find their way into print, just enough to keep up public interest, without giving the least idea of what was actually being done. All that was definitely known was that she was built of metal, upon lines that experience had proved to be the most desirable.

So well had the plans of the builder succeeded, that, when the boat was ready for the water, only himself, the manager of the syndicate and two or three trusted employes were conversant with the entire construction. She was launched in June, after considerable difficulty, because of the faulty construction of the cradle which had been built to carry her down the ways. As soon as she was in the water, work on fitting her out was begun. The best riggers and sailmakers in the country had been engaged. Nothing that experience had taught or science could suggest in this respect was left undone.

When completed, with every rope, block and sail in position, experts of all shades of opinion pronounced her perfect. She was, indeed, an ideal racing machine. Graceful as a swan, her appearance filled the yachtsmen who saw her with an enthusiasm that was communicated with such good effect to the general public through the medium of the newspapers that it became universal. Columns upon columns of description were written and eagerly devoured by the reading public. It was conceded on all sides that the acme of yacht building had been reached, and that a boat worthy to represent this country had been produced to meet the venturesome Englishman.

This feeling of enthusiasm and the confidence that it naturally inspired, was measurably increased when the boat was put to the test. She was given two or three private trials, and then pitted against the entire fleet of the foremost yachting organization of this country.

Her success was phenomenal. Nothing in all that vast fleet could approach her during the cruises from one port to another. As stiff as a house in heavy weather, she was as fast as a witch in a light wind. The newspapers detailed their expert reporters to follow the fleet during the cruise, and the glowing accounts of the new boat's wonderful performances that were printed kept public feeling keyed up to the highest pitch of enthusiasm.

After the cruise had ended, the boat was overhauled and prepared for a series of trial races. These trial races had been previously agreed upon, in order that no mistake should be made in the selection of the boat to protect the cup, providing the one constructed by the syndicate did not come up to expectations.

The boat chosen as the newcomer's competitor in these trial races was conceded to be the best previously constructed. She had beaten all comers at all times, and had successfully defended the trophy against an English boat in a series of the most exciting races ever sailed for the cup.

The outcome of the trial races was discounted by public opinion. The new boat succeeded in winning two of the three races in such a decisive manner as to leave no doubt in the mind of anyone as to which was the better yacht. She would have won all three were it not for the fact that, during the second race, she met with an accident that virtually crippled her.

The committee to which had been delegated the power of selection met, and, merely as a formality, publicly announced that the new boat had been chosen to represent this country in the international contest.

While the foregoing had been transpiring, the English boat had arrived on this side of the Atlantic. She crossed the ocean unaccompanied, and during the twenty-two days of the voyage had proved herself to be as seaworthy as she was fast. Her owner had also arrived, and from the deck of his boat had watched the trials of the two Americans. The English boat had many admirers among the thousands who inspected her, and it was admitted that she would prove at least a worthy rival.

Everything progressed smoothly as the dates for the international contests drew near. There was not a hitch in any of the arrangements, public interest had been maintained by detailed accounts of the almost daily spins of the two rivals, and all went as merrily as the proverbial marriage bell.

Shortly before the day set for the first race, in the first part of September, both boats were specially groomed for the fray. Rigging was overhauled, sails tried and set, blocks retested and everything made taut.

When the English boat arrived, it had been discovered that she did not have on board any of her fittings, water tanks, bulk-heads, etc. There was a rule of the club under which the races were to be decided, requiring yachts to sail in such races with their tanks, fittings, etc., on board, as when prepared for ord-inary use. To meet this exigency, a clause was inserted in the detailed agreement for the races, waiving this rule. In order that the American boat should not be placed at any disadvantage, it was decided to strip her also. Accordingly her fittings, tanks, bulkheads, etc., which she had carried in all the trial races, were removed. They were found to weigh in the neighborhood of 7,000 pounds. To replace this weight, three tons of pig lead were cut and placed in her hold.

Two tons were put in while she was at her anchorage. The remaining ton was placed in her just before she was officially measured. This ton was cut and stowed while she lay at anchor, near the starting point, the night before the date of the first race.

It had been agreed that the match should be the best three in five races, the courses for each race to be fixed by the regatta committee appointed to supervise the contests. Every arrange-ment had been perfected several days before the date set for the first race. The day previous to the first event the boats were measured by the official measurer of the yacht club and were found to be so evenly matched that there was a difference of only a few seconds in time allowance. This difference, by the way, was in favor of the American boat.

At last the impatiently awaited day arrived. Thousands of

sightseers, eager to watch the battle between the best yachts in the world, crowded every description of excursion boats. Hundreds of craft, from the great three-decked steamer to the tiniest tug, were clustered around the starting point when the contesting yachts arrived.

The weather was almost perfect for yachting, The sun shone brightly, the sea was calm, and the wind registered from five to eight miles an hour. Such a scene of enthusiasm as was witnessed when the two boats were sent away on their thirty mile trip will never be forgotten by those persons who were fortunate enough to be present. The echoes of the starting-gun were drowned by the shrill chorus of whistles from the steamers as the two racers, with every stitch of canvas spread, crossed the line.

It was a beautiful race, unmarred by anything approaching an untoward incident. The enthusiasm of the spectators, as the steamers accompanied the flying beauties, was unbounded at the start. It increased immeasurably as the race progressed, when it was observed that the American champion was proving herself the better boat. It reached an almost hysterical climax when, several hours later, the American boat, skimming like a bird over the surface of the water, crossed the finishing line about nine minutes ahead of her competitor.

The Englishman had been beaten, as had been anticipated, but he had not been disgraced. His boat had proved herself a wonder, and had caused even the most sanguine of partisans to express thankfulness that the American builder had succeeded in producing such a marvelous craft. It was realized that any of the boats previously built in this country would have been defeated.

It was, indeed, a most auspicious beginning to what promised to be the most famous contest ever held, and the committee having the affair in charge were congratulating themselves on that fact, when a change came over the scene.

That evening they received from the Englishman a request that both yachts be remeasured before the next race. Had lightning out of a clear sky landed in their midst, they would not have been more astonished. What did it mean? Could it be that the Englishman thought that the correct measurements had not been taken by the official measurer?

The knowledge that the Englishman had made such an unprecedented request flew like wild-fire from one end of the country to the other. The newspapers of the next day were filled with it. It was denounced on all sides as a slur on the honesty of American yachtsmen, that should be met with the most vigorous resentment. Some even went so far as to counsel that the Englishman be forced to indite an apology before the next race should be sailed.

The details of the controversy that had arisen were carefully guarded. Everybody connected with the affair declined to talk, but it was formally announced that evening that the request of the Englishman had been granted, and that both yachts would be remeasured.

Despite the fact that the day following the first race was Sunday, the official measurer of the yacht club visited the boats and remeasured them. It was found, to the satisfaction of everyone, that the load water line of the American boat did not differ materially from the measurements taken before the first race. By agreement, each boat was marked on the load water line. This apparently settled the question, and, though the feeling of resentment occasioned by the Englishman's request had not entirely disappeared, preparations were made for the second race, which was scheduled to be sailed the following Tuesday.

Public feeling had been aroused by the action of the Englishman to such an extent, that the rush to witness the second race was even greater than that which had taken place on the first day.

Unfortunately, while manœuvring for a start, a foul occurred by which the American boat was the greatest sufferer. Soon after crossing the line, when it was discovered that material damage had been inflicted to the rigging, the American boat hoisted a protest flag, claiming a foul. Both boats continued over the course, the Englishman winning by the small margin of fifty-seven seconds, corrected time.

After the race, the representative of the American boat lodged a formal protest with the race committee. The committee, after due deliberation, decided that the English boat had broken Section 11 of Rule 16 of the rules of racing, and awarded the race to the American boat.

This, of course, gave rise to a great deal of discussion, and the excitement of the public grew apace. It was as nothing, however, to what followed.

The next race was scheduled for Thursday. Both boats appeared at the starting point, ready for the battle. The gun was fired, the crowds on the excursion boats cheered. Everything indicated a great contest. To the great surprise of the people, however, the English boat, after crossing the line, turned about and headed for her anchorage, leaving the American boat to go over the course alone. This she did, and was afterward formally awarded the race.

The feeling engendered by the action of the English boat was bitter.   Nor was it lessened to any extent when it was publicly announced that the Englishman had refused to compete in the third race, because he was convinced that he would not be accorded a clear field by the excursion boats.   He was denounced on all sides and declared no sportsman.

The unhappy circumstances attending the outcome of what had at first promised to be one of the greatest sporting events of the century had about been dismissed from the public mind, when the yachting world was startled by the publication, in an English paper, of charges made by the owner of the English yacht, reflecting on the integrity of the managers of the American boat.

The charges were, briefly, that the American boat was more deeply immersed on the day of the first race than she was when she was measured on the day previous, or on the day following, when she was remeasured.   It was contended that this fact gave her an undue advantage.   The Englishman did not pretend to account for the change in the water line that he claimed he had observed, but indicated that it must necessarily have been caused by a manipulation of ballast.

These charges were a great surprise to the American public. Nothing of the nature had ever been hinted at, even when the Englishman had requested that the yachts be remeasured.   The effect was startling, and a demand for public retraction of the charges was made by every newspaper in the country.

So persistent was the demand that the yacht club, under whose auspices the races had been sailed, at the request of the members of the syndicate owning the American boat, appointed a committee to investigate the charges.

Three of the most prominent men in the country were chosen, and they, acting within the power granted them by the yacht club, added two more equally prominent gentlemen to the committee. Complete, it was as august a court as ever convened to consider any question. It had no standing, in a judicial sense, of course, and could not compel witnesses to testify under oath, but nevertheless the high character of its members made it certain that its investigation would be fairly and satisfactorily conducted.

Within a few weeks all preliminaries had been completed and the investigation begun. It was conducted behind closed doors, and the members of the committee, as well as the witnesses called, were pledged to secrecy. The owner of the English boat had made the trip to this country, accompanied by his counsel, especially for the purpose of reiterating the charges in person. He was the first to be heard.

Through his counsel, he made a detailed statement of the position he had taken in the controversy. He claimed that the charges he had been called upon to prove were not new. That they had been made to a representative of the committee on the day of the first race. In an affidavit submitted he stated in part: . . .

"On the day before the first race I saw the American boat. I . . . looked at the port side . . . and specially noticed an outlet hole about midships, which was just cut by the water, a little above the base. . . . I also distinctly noticed the line of bronze plating, and also the bobstay bolt. . . . On the morning of the day of the first race I was awakened . . . and requested to look at the American boat. I looked at her carefully through a pair of glasses and I was convinced that she

was lying deeper in the water than when measured. . . .
When I went to put . . . on board the American boat my
representative, . . . I inspected her with great care to see
whether the pipe hole and other marks which I had previously
observed were in the same position as when she was measured.
The outlet hole on the port side was nowhere visible above the
water, and in my judgment and belief the line of bronze plating
and bobstay bolt were nearer to the water than when she was
measured. . . . I came to the conclusion, which I still believe to be a true conclusion, that the vessel was immersed three
or four inches deeper in the water than when she was measured. . . .

"When a member of the committee came on board my
boat as a representative of the American yacht, I stated that I
was sure that the American boat was not sailing on her measured
length, but was more deeply immersed. . . . I said that I
wished the committee to put one of their members, or some reliable representative on board each of the yachts immediately
after the race, and that they should be remeasured the same
evening, if possible, but if that were impossible, that the representatives of the committee remain on board the yachts until
remeasurement took place. . . . Immediately after the race,
I put the American representative on board the committee boat
for the purpose of laying my complaint and requests before the
committee. . . I received no communication from the
committee. . . . Both vessels were remeasured on the following afternoon and their load water line was found to be the
same as when originally measured. . . ."

After the reading of the affidavit, the counsel for the manager
of the American syndicate examined the Englishman at length,

with reference to the question of deeper immersion and the possible means of securing it. The examination proceeded as follows:

Q.—Did you form any idea . . . of how much deeper she was in the water than when measured ? A.—Three or four inches, I think. . . .

Q.—Does not your judgment involve the conclusion on your part that twelve or fourteen tons had been secretly been put on board of her? A.—No, certainly not.

Q.—How much ? A.—If you assume that the alteration in immersion was made by lead, and take my lowest estimate of three inches, . . . it would take about nine or ten tons. I have nowhere stated that I believed that the immersion was caused by the introduction of ballast—lead.

Q.—Introduction of something ? A.—Introduction of something . . .

Q.—But you never formed any idea as to what was introduced ? A.—No.

Q.—But your belief was that some substance or substances to the amount of nine or ten tons had been secretly introduced into her after she was measured . . . ? A.—Yes. . . .

Q.—Did you think that nine or ten tons of material could be loaded . . . without its being known to a considerable number of people? A.—Lead could not be loaded, of course. . . . I presume water might be introduced without its being known to a number of people.

Q.—Did you believe that water had been introduced ? A.— I really had no opinion as to what was done. . . .

Examined by his own counsel as to the probable reason for the American boat being more deeply immersed on the day of the first race, the Englishman testified as follows:

Q.—Had there been a wind blowing strongly the evening before the day of the first race? A.—Yes.

Q.—Was there an appearance of heavy weather the next day? A.—Yes; we expected a hard wind the next day.

Q.—Was that the kind of weather in which, in your opinion, it would be of advantage for the American boat to be immersed more deeply? A.—Yes.

Several affidavits of persons who had been connected in an official capacity with the English boat were introduced by counsei, for the purpose of showing that the apparent deeper immersion of the American yacht had been observed by others besides the Englishman. One, made by the official sailmaker of the English boat, contained the following statement:

" . . . I carefully observed the American boat when the measurement, on the day previous to the first race, was made. . . . I distinctly saw that the load water line intersected the outlet of a pipe as nearly as possible amidships. . . . On the morning of the next day (while the yachts were lying in open water), I noticed that the American boat was lying lower in the water than she had previously been. . . . I . . . got into a boat and rowed up to the American yacht to look at her closely, . . . and the pipe before mentioned was nowhere to be seen. . . ."

Another, from the sailing master of the English boat, said in part:

" . . . I saw the American yacht a day or two after the last trial race. . Paid great attention to her water line and trim, and . . . no pipe hole was then visible on her port side. I saw her again the day she was measured for the first race. . She was very much lighter, . . .

and I then observed a pipe hole on the port side amidships.
. . . It was plainly visible just above the water line. I again
saw her (on the day of the first race). . . . I was not near
enough to see the pipe hole, but . . . she was lower in the
water. I again saw her when she was remeasured . . .
and then again I saw the pipe hole on the port side."

Another, from a personal friend of the English owner,
stated in part:

" . . . On the day before the first race (while the American boat was being measured), I distinctly saw a pipe hole in
the port side amidships. . . . On (the next day) . . . I
rowed around the American boat . . . I saw distinctly she
was at that time much deeper in the water than when she was
measured. I looked for the pipe hole, . . . and it was then
covered by the water and could not be seen. . . . Both
yachts were remeasured (the day after the race). . . . I then
saw the pipe hole showing above the water, in exactly the same
manner as it did when the boat was first measured, and the
yacht appeared to be at that time in exactly the same trim as
when she was first measured. . . ."

The gentleman was examined by counsel for both sides, but
no further statements of material importance were elicited. A
number of affidavits from seamen on board the English yacht,
were then submitted to show that unusual activity was noticeable on the American yacht during the night preceding the day
of the first race.

This ended the case for the English owner, his counsel ad-
mitting that "we do not propose to go into the question of at-
tempting, without evidence which we cannot *now* obtain, to
attack statements which we have no material to investigate."

Counsel for the manager of the American syndicate, in his opening address, outlined the policy of the defense, in which it was proposed to prove "incontestably, if any human evidence can be relied on, that there is no foundation for the charges," . . . that the opinions expressed by the Englishmen were due to a mere delusion or illusion, by which it appeared that the American boat was more deeply immersed on the day of the first race than she was on the day she was measured.

The designer and builder of the American yacht was the first witness called. After being interrogated as to the design and build of the boat, he was examined by counsel for the defense as follows:

Q.—Can you tell . . . how much additional weight would have to be placed in her to immerse her four inches deeper in the water (than she was when she was first measured ?) . . . A.—Four inches would require 28,541 pounds (about fourteen short tons). . . .

In answer to questions, the designer stated that three tons of lead ballast had been placed in the hold of the American boat, before she was officially measured, to take the place of the water tanks, and other articles removed from her when she was stripped for the races.

Q.—Was there any possibility of any water ballast, or any other ballast, being used on her that day (the day of the first race), except these three tons of lead ? A.—No, certainly not.

Q.—Could you tell . . . if there had been ten or fourteen tons of extra weight put into her ? Would you have recognized it as she sailed ? A.—Yes; I think I would.

Q.—How would it have affected her . . .? A.—There would be quite a difference to her motion in a seaway.

Q.—When you went on board (on the morning of the day of the first race), . . . did you see any difference in . . . her immersion or the load water length? A.—Of course, when all the crew were on board, with all their cots, that put her down somewhat in the water.

Q.—The . . . crew were on her when she was measured, were they not? A.—Oh, yes.

Q.—Was there any appreciable weight or difference occasioned by the cots? A.—No, . . . There would be very little difference in the trim. . . .

Q.—Had you observed the weather the night before? A.— Yes. . . . The wind was fresh, east, and had the appearance of being a strong breeze the next day. We expected a stormy day. . . .

Q.—(By member of committee.)—What was this hole in the side we hear so much of? A.—It was the delivery to the bilge pump.   . It was intended to be just above the water line.

Q.—(By counsel for Englishman.)—Do I understand that the cots were on board (when you arrived on the boat, between 8 and 9 o'clock on the morning of the day of the race)? A.— I do not remember whether they were on board then or not. . . .

When the committee convened for the second day's session the designer of the American boat was recalled and further examined by counsel for the manager of the American syndicate.

Q.—You spoke yesterday of a leak in the boat, will you tell what it amounted to? A.— . . . I don't know the exact amount—probably twenty or thirty gallons (a day). . . . When she was under sail she leaked a little more.

Q.— . . . How much (would) a list of one degree change the position of the water pipe in relation to the water line? A.—Well, . . . heeling her one degree would immerse her side amidships something over two inches.

Q.—How much weight would it take to do that? A.— . . About one-half or . . . three-quarters of a ton.

Q.—(By member of committee.)—Did you say whether the tanks had been taken out of the boat? A.—Yes.

Q.—What was the capacity of those tanks? A.—I think the water tank had a capacity of some six or seven hundred gallons. I don't remember exactly. . . . There was a water tank and a waste tank into which the water ran from basins and was pumped overboard. That was taken out. That was much smaller. And there was also a large wooden tank, lined with zinc, for the storage of ice.

Q.—That was taken out, too? A.—Yes.

Q.—Do you know how much a gallon of sea-water weighs? A.—I don't remember exactly the proportion; it is about eight and a half pounds, I think, roughly; sixty-four and three-tenths pounds to the cubic yard.

Q.—(By member of committee.)—Is there any place beside the hold where ballast could have been secreted without being exposed to ordinary observation? A.—No.

In answer to further questioning by members of the committee, the witness testified that if all of the crew of the boat were on one side it would give her a list of about three or four inches. He was on deck when the Englishman rowed around the boat to put his representative on board. He could not remember the number of persons standing on deck on that side (the port) when the Englishman arrived.

The representative of the regatta committee, who had been on board the English yacht during the races, was then called and examined by counsel for the manager of the syndicate. He gave a detailed account of the conversation between himself and the owner of the English boat regarding the statement that the American boat was not sailing on her measured load water line.

Q.—Did he (the Englishman) ask or say that he wished the committee to put one of its members, or some reliable representative, on board of each yacht immediately after the race, . . . to stay on board in charge of the vessels until they were remeasured? A.—No, sir.

In answer to further interrogations, he stated that he had laid the complaint before the committee immediately after the race, and that the committee had ordered a remeasurement the next day.

The owner of the English boat was then recalled and further examined. He reiterated his statement that he had requested the committee to place some one in charge of the boats until they were remeasured.

Q.—(By English counsel.)—This race was looked upon as a very important race and there was a good deal of money on it? A.—I believe so.

Q.—Which money was of importance, and might be the reason of——? A.—(Interrupting.)—I believe there was a great deal of betting on it.

At the close of the morning session the English owner bid the committee adieu and sailed that afternoon for England. His counsel remained behind to attend to his interests until the investigation should end.

At the afternoon session a personal friend of the manager of the syndicate, who had sailed on the American boat from the time she was launched, was called. In answer to inquiries he stated that the American boat had sailed without any ballast in the hold during all the trial races. He corroborated former witnesses in stating that the 3,000 pounds of lead had been put in prior to the date of the first measurement to take the place of the tanks and furniture that had been taken out of the boat. He stated that the owner of the boat made it a practice to inspect the hold of the vessel personally every day. He could not state the reason for such personal inspection, but was of the opinion that it was not made with the idea of detecting any attempt at fraud.

Another friend of the manager was then called. He was a civil engineer and surveyor and had measured the American boat some time after the races. She was then stripped of everything and was considerably lighter than when in racing trim. His measurement had shown that the racing line or load water line, which had been officially marked after the first race, was then six and one-fourth inches above the water. He did not see any ballast in her. He had noticed that there were three pipe holes on the starboard side and two pipe holes on the port side. He found all the pipe holes lower than the line indicated by the marks made by the official measurer, giving the load water line.

The manager of the American boat was then called to the stand. He testified that his first intimation that the owner of the English boat had made a complaint was had when he read a newspaper report to that effect more than a month after the races. He had heard absolutely nothing concerning the complaint before that time. He told in detail what had been done with the boat on the days previous to the sailing of the first race. He had not noticed any difference in her trim when he boarded her on the morning of the day of the race.

Q.—(By his counsel.)—You attended the remeasurement on the day following the race ? A.—Yes. . . .

Q.—To your knowledge had anything been taken out of her or let out of her in any way from the time she started on the race until then ? A.—Nothing, to my knowledge. . . .

Q.—I will ask you . . . whether any such thing could have occurred as has been suggested—either the lightening of the boat preliminary to the first measurement, the putting on board in any form of any weight to the extent of nine or ten tons, or to any amount, and the taking it out again before the second measurement, without your knowledge ? A.—I cannot imagine that such a thing could be possible. . . .

Q.—(By counsel for Englishman.)—This furniture and these traps and tanks (that were taken out of the boat before the first measurement) must have weighed a great deal. Did you keep on adding to them in a casual manner, without testing the weight that was actually in the boat, or did you fit her up with a certain number of tanks and a certain amount of furniture, and not add to those during the summer ? A.—They were not added to during the summer.

Q.—In any of the races, at the time when she was fitted up with her furniture, did you stiffen her at times by loose ballast ? A.—Never. . . .

Q.—When you examined the boat on the morning of the day of the first race, where did you look at her hold ? A.—Two different places, aft and about midships. I mean to say aft, that is, coming down just at the bottom of the companion-way.

Q.—Where was the lead stowed? A.— . . . Right on top of the keel and between her frames.

Q.—Whereabouts in the boat? A.—Well, it was a little aft of midships. Part of the lead was a little aft of a partition that came between the sail room and cabin, which partition was left at that time. . . .

Q.—If the statement that the boat was sailing more deeply immersed than when she had been measured . . . had been known to you, it would have been a matter . . . which would affect the race. Your boat would have been disqualified, I presume, if it had been found out to be the fact? A.—Yes, if it had been found out so. . . .

Q.—The tanks upon the boat were movable tanks? A.— You could get them out, yes.

Q.—Were they fixed tanks, according to the design? . . . A.—They were put in there so that they could be taken out any time we wanted to. . . . They were under the cabin floor.

The sailing master of the American boat, who was with her from the time she was launched until after the races, was then called as a witness. He corroborated what had been said about taking out the tanks and furniture and putting in the three tons of lead. He testified that between the time when the boat was officially measured and the start for the race the next day, he had been on board in charge. Nothing in the way of ballast had been taken on board the boat after she was measured, and nothing had been taken off except the cots and bedding of the sailors, which had been used during the night. He also testified that to his positive knowledge, nothing had been taken out of the boat during the night following the day of the race and preceding the measurement the day following.

Q.—(By counsel for manager of syndicate.)—What do you say to the suggestion that before the measurement on Friday she was lightened to make her set more out of the water, that after the measurement nine or ten tons of some heavy substance was carried on board of her to immerse her deeper in the water, and as much taken out of her before the remeasurement to restore her to her original condition? A.—I say that there is not a word of truth in it. There was no such thing done. . . .

Q.—Had you noticed the discharge from the pipe on the port side when the boat was under way, sailing? A.— . . . I don't remember. . . .

Q.—Did you notice it at that time (the morning of the day of the first race)? A.—I don't remember that morning particularly. . . .

Q.—(By counsel for Englishman.)—How big was the pump for this hole? A.—I could not say what was the size of the pump.

Q.—Were there any other pumps in the boat? . . . A.—Water closet pumps. There is always a pump connected with a water closet.

Q.—Had there been a water closet forward on the starboard side? A.—Yes, sir.

Q.—Was that water closet taken out or not? A.—No.

Q.—How many water closets were left in? A.—Four, . . two on the port side and two on the starboard side.

Q.—You had three on the starboard side, had you not? A.—Yes, sir. . . . I want to say, gentlemen, that that boat sailed those races with just every pound of weight aboard of her that she was measured with, and not a pound more.

Several members of the regatta committee, which had

charge of the details of the contests, were examined. Their testimony was all against the supposition that the American boat had carried more ballast of any kind on the day of the race than she had when first measured. Their testimony also showed that their representative, who had sailed on the English boat, had not made known to them the request, claimed to have been made by the English owner, that the boats should be taken in charge by members of the committee or a reliable representative, until they were remeasured the following day.

The next witness to be examined was the carpenter who had been employed on the American boat during all the time she was in commission. He described fully what had been done on board the boat during the days preceding the first race, corroborating preceding witnesses in all essential details.

Q.—(By counsel for manager of syndicate.)—Did you know of any place in that vessel where water ballast . . . could have been stowed without your knowing it? A.—No, sir. It would have been impossible to put it there. There was no place to put it.

Q.—Nothing to hold water? A.—There was nothing to hold water except the hull of the boat. The water would have to enter the bilge, if any water was carried aboard.

Q.—From your knowledge . . . was there anything taken into her or out of her (during the days preceding and following the race), except the three tons of lead and the cots of the men? A.—No, sir; there was not.

The assistant sailing master of the American boat was then examined at length. His knowledge of what had taken place on board the vessel during the time covered by the investigation was complete in consequence of the fact that he had not been away from her more than an hour at any time. His testimony concerning the amount of lead ballast put into the boat and the impossibility of shifting ballast to or from the boat during the time between the first and second measurements, was stronger even than that of previous witnesses.

Q.—(By counsel for manager of syndicate.)—Was there anything taken out, poured out, or left out of the boat (from the time she started in the race until she was remeasured?) A.—No, sir.

Q.—Could there have been without you knowing it? A.—I don't think it could have been done; no, sir.

The first mate of the boat was then examined along the same lines as previous witnesses. His testimony was mainly corroborative. He had been employed on the boat since the day she was launched.

Q.—(By counsel for manager of syndicate.)—You had become by this time pretty familiar with the boat, had you not? A.—With the upper part of her; yes, sir. From the deck, I mean.

The second mate was then interrogated. He stated that he was familiar with the hold of the vessel and had been instructed to look for water in the bilge several times during the race. He had gone below three or four times and had not discovered any water.

Q.—(By counsel for Englishman.)—Did you notice the pump by the bilge amidships? There was a pump there? A.—Yes, sir; there is a pump there.

Q.—What size is it? A.—Well, I never took exact notice, but I should say it was an inch and a quarter discharge.

Q.—Is there a pump forward? A.—No bilge pump forward; no, sir.

Q.—Is there a pump forward? A.—This pump was about midships.

Q.—I know, but was there another pump forward? A.—No, sir.

Q.—Was there a pump on the starboard side forward? A.—No, sir.

Q.—There was a pipe hole there, was there not, on the starboard side, forward? A.—There is a pipe hole to the closet.

Q.—Was there a pump there? A.—There was no bilge pump to pump the ship out with.

Q.—Was there a pump? A.—A water-closet pump, that is all.

Q.—Was that all the pump that was forward on the starboard side? A.—Yes, sir.

Affidavits from members of the crew containing evidence corroborative of previous witnesses and tending to prove the charges made by the Englishman to have been without foundation in fact were submitted to the committee and ordered placed on the minutes.

The first witness called at the last day's session of the committee was the captain of the barge that had acted as a tender to the American yacht during the time she was in commission for the races. His testimony was slightly different from that given by previous witnesses.

Q.—(By counsel for manager of syndicate.)—You were captain of the tender? A.—Yes, sir.

Q.—Have you brought with you her log of (the time covered by this investigation?) A.—No, sir; I have not.

Q.—Where is it? A.—I have got it home.

Q.—Were you not requested to bring it? A.—Well, now,

gentlemen, I will tell you.   I wrote that for my own benefit, and I wrote it for the purpose of publishing a book.   That is what I have kept it for.   .   .   .   That is the reason why I didn't bring it.   .

Q.—I wish   .   .   .   you would   .   .   .   give the movements of the tender during (the time that elapsed between the first measurement of the American boat and the measurement after the first race?)   A.—Well, if that is going to be published in the paper, I don't think I ought to tell.   .   .   .   I don't want to injure myself.

Q.—The committee is entitled to have it from you.   A.—I know I have done everything for the committee.   I have been told to keep my mouth shut and I have kept it shut.   I have been offered $75 by the newspapers to publish it long ago and I wouldn't do it, because I was told to keep my mouth shut.   .   .   .   They told me not to say anything.   I have had outside parties come to me to keep still, and I have done it.   .   .   .

Q.—From the time the boat was first measured to the time she was remeasured on the day following the first race, do you know of anything being put into her or taken out of her except the men's cots and clothes and bags?   A.—Ask me any other question, and I am willing to answer anything that won't injure me any.   .   .   .

Q.—(By counsel for Englishman.)—When you stripped the boat before the races, do you remember what pumps were left inside of her?   A.—I don't know how many pumps she had on to her.

Q.—Did you see any pumps?   A.—I don't know.   I never went down and examined the boat inside.

Q.—Did you never go down inside the boat?   A.—I have

been in her lots of times and been all through her. . . .

Q.—Have you seen her building plans ? A.—I think I did, yes, sir.

Q.—Where ? A.— . . . I don't think I ought to answer that question. . . . I don't think it's any of my business to say that.

The captain of the tender was finally dismissed, and the sailing master of the American yacht recalled and further interrogated. His testimony touched on the impossibility of having the yacht remeasured on the evening following the first race.

Q.—(By counsel for Englishman.)—Was there a bilge pump connected with this hole in the port side amidships ? A.—There was. . . . The pumps operated from the deck.

Q.—Was there any pump connected with this hole on the starboard side forward, that we have heard of ? A.—Water closet pump. That is a permanent fixture there. . . .

Q.—There was no bilge pump there ? A.—Not at all; only one bilge pump in the boat.

The official measurer of the yachts was then called to identify some drawings of the boat that had been made. This ended the taking of testimony and the committee announced that the investigation was closed. It was determined by the committee that they should visit the yacht as she lay in winter quarters. This was done, the counsel for the English owner accompanying them. An investigation of the interior of the boat, satisfactory to everyone concerned, was made, and the committee devoted itself to the preparation of its report. The report was formally presented about three weeks after the investigation closed.

In the report the committee carefully reviewed all the evi-

dence, oral and written, that had been submitted. The argument throughout was essentially unprejudiced, each fact and
each statement receiving due consideration and given due
weight. Whatever slight discrepancies in detail had been discovered on revision were reconciled, and rough places made
smooth. As a matter of fact, the evidence produced by the
manager of the syndicate had been surprisingly uniform, due,
perhaps, to the able manner in which his counsel had, by adroit
questioning, kept his witnesses from wandering from a well-
defined, beaten path.

After summing up the evidence and weighing it thoroughly,
the committee stated:

" Upon a careful consideration of the whole case, the committee are unanimously of the opinion that the charge made by
the English owner (that the American boat sailed the first race immersed about three or four inches more than she was when first
measured, and therefore, on a longer load water line) and which
has been the subject of this investigation, had its origin in mistake;
that it is not only not sustained by evidence, but is completely
disproved; and that all the circumstances indicated by him as
giving rise to his suspicion, are entirely and satisfactorily explained. They deem it, therefore, but just to the gentlemen
connected with the American boat, as well as to the officers and
crew, that the committee should express emphatically their con-
viction that nothing whatever occurred in connection with the
race in question that casts the least suspicion upon the integrity
or propriety of their conduct. . . . And they ask to be dis-
charged from further consideration of the subject referred to
them."

The report was received with every evidence of satisfaction

by the public and was unanimously adopted by the yacht club. It closed a decidedly unpleasant incident in the history of yachting, and the subject was dismissed. To indicate its sentiments in a more forceful manner, the yacht club expelled the Englishman from honorary membership, an action which met with a popular expression of the sentiment that it "served him right."

———————

Several years elapsed, and during that time the affair had almost faded from the public mind. All reference to the controversy had been carefully avoided in the press, and those persons who had been actively connected with it had discreetly refrained from mentioning it, either in public or private. It was considered for the best interests of the sport to obliterate it, as far as possible.

This plan had succeeded to such an extent that the announcement that the case was to be reopened on behalf of the English owner caused widespread surprise. The intelligence came without warning, but ample opportunity was given those interested to become familiar with the details of the proposed proceeding before the investigation began.

It is needless to say that the finding of the court of inquiry which conducted the first investigation had not met with the approval of some persons whose conceptions of right and justice were not overshadowed by partisan feelings. The English owner and his most intimate friends had apparently accepted the verdict. At least, they had not given any public expression of disapproval. They were, to all appearances, content to leave the case as it stood.

There were some persons, however, who had become

deeply interested in the controversy, who had determined to investigate the matter for themselves. Without informing the English owner of their intentions, they proceeded quietly to gather whatever evidence bearing on the question it was possible to procure. They had not proceeded with their quest far before they became convinced that a grave mistake had been made somewhere.

Progress was naturally slow. The greatest obstacles had to be overcome and the most scrupulous care was absolutely necessary to prevent any intimation of the search becoming known to the parties on either side. Patience was at last rewarded, however, and about three years after the date of the events recorded above the case was completed.

Extensive preparations were made for its presentation. An eminent counsel, who had become familiar with the subject, was retained to conduct the case. Papers were prepared and all was in readiness when the announcement was made.

The court which convened at the hearing was the most remarkable ever called to adjudicate any question. It included prominent representatives of all the English-speaking nations of the earth. In addition, interpreters of all known languages were engaged, in order that the proceedings might be translated and read by the peoples of every country in the world.

Contrary to the method of procedure of the former court of inquiry, every effort was made to give the facts brought out the widest publicity.

When the proceedings began, thousands of persons were interested spectators. The doors were thrown wide open. Nothing was done in secret. All who were interested in the matter were able to hear the testimony. After a few prelimina-

ries, made necessary by the extraordinary nature of the proceedings, the eminent counsel began his opening address. He
said:

"May it please the court, the case which I now desire to
present for your consideration, though complete in itself, is essentially a part of one which has previously been passed upon
by a court of inquiry formed for the purpose of adjudicating it.
As a matter of fact, it may be properly described as a continua-
tion of that case.

"The case referred to was the outcome of a controversy
arising from certain charges made by the owner of the English
yacht which was the contestant in a series of races arranged to
be sailed for a trophy, the possession of which is conceded to
represent supremacy in the professions of boat building and
seamanship. The honorable court is presumably familiar with
the published facts of the controversy referred to, but for the
purpose of obviating any possibility of a misunderstanding, I
beg leave to touch lightly upon the important incidents which
led up to it.

"During the month of November, 1694, an English sportsman, who had been prominently identified with the sport of
yachting, issued a challenge for a series of races with an American boat, for the purpose of endeavoring to regain possession of
a cup, known as the International Trophy, which had been won
by an American boat several years previously, and had remained
in the possession of American yachtsmen, despite numerous
attempts to win it back.

"After some trifling delay, his challenge was accepted, and
arrangements made for the contests, which, it was agreed, were
to take place during the month of September, 1695. I will not

refer to the incidents which occurred during the time which elapsed from the acceptance of the challenge to the date of the first contest.   They have no material bearing upon the case at this time.

"Naturally, an event of such widespread interest and really international importance, created more than the ordinary amount of public feeling and discussion, and naturally, also, more than the ordinary amount of speculation as to the outcome.   The boats were apparently very evenly matched, and this fact caused considerable money to be placed upon the result.   There is no way in which even an approximate estimate of the amount wagered by individuals can be made, but it was common gossip in the clubs and in the exchanges that thousands of dollars were at stake.

"I call the court's attention to this fact, not for the purpose of intimating that it had any effect on what transpired later, but entirely with a view to indicating the vast amount of interest taken in the contests.

"On the morning of the day set for the first contest, the owner of the English boat became convinced that the American boat was more deeply immersed than she had been the day previous, when she was measured by the official measurer of the yacht club, under whose auspices the races were to be sailed.   The boats were lying close together, near where the starting point for that day's race was to be staked off.

"In order that he might observe the vessel more closely, to prevent any possible chance for mistake that might arise from an inspection at a distance, the Englishman entered a small boat and rowed around the American yacht.   From this inspection, he became assured that his suspicion was well founded.

"When the gentleman who, according to the established custom, was to sail on the English boat that day as a representative of the yacht club arrived, the English owner informed him of the suspicions aroused by the appearance of the American boat. He requested the representative to lay a complaint before the regatta committee, and requested that both yachts be remeasured that night, after the race. If remeasurement that night was deemed impracticable, he then requested that members of the committee or reliable representatives be placed in charge of the boats until such time as they could be remeasured.

"The first part of his request was granted. The second was not. The boats were remeasured the following day, but during the time that elapsed between the ending of the race and the remeasurement, none of the committee nor any representative was on either vessel.

" cite this request and the manner in which it was treated merely as indicating the feeling which prevailed even at that time against the English owner. Had it been granted in its entirety and representatives placed on board the yachts until they were remeasured, we are positive, from what knowledge we have gained, that the final result would not have been in the least degree affected.

"The American boat was remeasured the following day, and her load water line was found to be within a fraction of an inch of the figures obtained at the first measurement.

"The contests which followed need not be referred to. They have no material reference to the matter under consideration.

" The fact that the English owner had asked for a remeasurement of the yachts, thereby indicating a suspicion that something was wrong, gained wide publicity through the newspapers and created considerable feeling among the people. To avoid, as much as possible, further public discussion of the matter, the English owner and the members of the regatta committee arrived at an agreement that nothing should be stated in reference to the load water line of the American boat in any of the official reports made upon the races.

"He left for home with this understanding. In the latter part of the following month of October, he read a report of the regatta committee in which the load water line question was specifically referred to. In answer to the statements contained in the report, he issued a pamphlet in which his side of the case was stated. A portion of this pamphlet was reprinted in an English sporting paper and gained wide publicity.

"As a result of the discussion which the publications engendered, an investigation of the matter was ordered by the yacht club. A court of inquiry, composed of prominent gentlemen, was convened. The Englishman, accompanied by his counsel, appeared before the court, and gave such evidence as was then in his possession to prove that his suspicion concerning the American boat was correct. The evidence was founded almost entirely upon the judgment formed by himself and others associated with him by the appearance of the American boat on the morning of the day of the first race. His contention was that between the time the boat was first measured and the time he saw her on the following morning, a great amount of ballast, approximating nine or ten tons, had been introduced, thereby increasing her immersion and lengthening her load water line. He offered nothing more tangible than the evidence of his own eyesight and the judgment of himself and others in support of his contention.

"The defense was thorough. Numberless witnesses were examined, and by their testimony it was proved to the satisfaction of the court that nothing but the proper amount of ballast had been put in the boat. The finding of the court was in accordance with the weight of evidence, and can be summed up in the following words:

"'Upon a careful consideration of the whole case, the committee are unanimously of the opinion that the charge . . . had its origin in mistake; that it is not only not sustained by evidence, but is completely disproved. . . .'

"And so the case ended. Now, may it please the court, it is not contended that any other verdict could have been rendered on the evidence produced at that hearing of the case. But since that time there has been secured evidence that, in our opinion, justifies this action for a rehearing.

"The court of inquiry asserted that 'the charge had its origin in mistake.' We propose to prove that it had, but that the mistake was not made by the English owner.

"We claim, and shall later on produce evidence to substantiate that claim, that the American boat was what is known in yachting parlance as a 'trick boat.' That she was so constructed that, by means of tanks effectually hidden from the view of even an expert, and pipes leading thereto, and a pump attachment, water ballast to the amount of 23,870 pounds, or about eleven tons, could be introduced and taken out at will.

"It is, perhaps, preferable that I should here briefly state the conclusions that we have arrived at, based upon the evidence that has been obtained. The evidence in the nature of the testimony, affidavits and drawings will be submitted later.

"The greatest secrecy was observed in the construction of

the boat.   She was built entirely of metal, and iron pipes, about two inches in diameter, were inserted between the frames. This created considerable surprise among the workmen engaged upon her, but their suspicions were allayed by the assertion that the pipes were put in to strengthen her.   Among the other peculiarities of the design from which she was built were iron frames, or braces, which extended from the keel to the floor of the hold.   These braces were fastened to the frames on the sides of the boat.   Holes were bored in the bottoms, through which the bilge water could run.   They were twenty inches apart.

"When she left the yard where she was built, these braces extended fore and aft, from one end of the boat to the other, with the exception of two spaces, one forward and one aft, where tanks for the holding of drinking and waste water were located.   These tanks were movable.   They could be taken out at will, and braces, similar to those used in the other sections, could be inserted.

"After she had been removed to the anchorage selected for her, two steel tanks were made for her.   The tanks were taken on board in sections.   The braces in the midship section of the lower hold were removed and the tanks fitted in their place. They were firmly fastened to the side frames and keel, and extended from the keel to the floor of the first hold.   When in position, they were directly underneath the steward's compartment, where were located the ranges or stoves on which the cooking for the crew was done.

"These tanks measured 385 cubic feet, and were capable of holding about 2,880 gallons of water.   This would be equal to 23,870 pounds, or about eleven tons.   After the tanks had been put in position, the men who had been employed on them were sent back to the yards and were not again allowed below decks.   A plumber who resided in a distant city was then engaged to make a connection with two of the iron pipes which had been placed between the frames of the boat for the purpose, as avowed, of strengthening her.

"One of these pipes was then connected with what is known as a 'syphon pump,' The pump had been procured at another distant city and placed in a compartment on the starboard side of the vessel, forward, which compartment had been constructed to resemble the water closets on the boat.   It could not, of course, be used as a water closet, and was kept locked.

"The plan was ingeniously devised, and so adroitly executed that not one of the men who had been employed to carry it out was cognizant of its entire scope.   Each had an idea of what was being done, but not one of them was able to comprehend how the scheme was to be worked.

"When completed, it was almost impossible for anyone to discover the existence of the tanks in the vessel.   The floor of the hold, with the exception of the midship section, was a series of hatches, which could be readily removed.   But even when this was done, as often happened when it was necessary to clean out the bilge, the tanks would not be noticed.   The ends of the tanks resembled so closely the braces which were in the forward and aft sections, that no distinction could be noticed.   The flooring of the steward's compartment, which rested on the tops of the tanks, was covered with sheet-iron. This, of course, could not be removed.

"Another peculiarity of the design on which the boat was constructed was the fact that her water line was seven inches

above her true water line.   The advantage of such an arrange-
ment is readily apparent.

"It was announced from the beginning that the boat was
designed to be sailed without any loose ballast.   All weight
thought necessary to give her a load water line within the limit
of ninety feet imposed by the conditions was introduced in a
leaden keel.   This keel weighed about eighty-five tons.

"The attention of this honorable court need not be called
to the great advantage accorded the boat by the possession of
the tanks described.   It can be easily understood.   In heavy
weather, when the wind blew strongly, the tanks would be
filled with water by removing the plug or cut-off from the inlet
pipe.   This would increase the ballast to the extent, as before
mentioned, of about eleven tons, enabling the boat to more
nearly retain an even keel, and at the same time a larger spread
of canvas than would have been possible without such increase
in ballast.   In so-called light weather, when only a fair sailing
breeze prevailed, the water, by means of the pump, could be
removed from the tanks, and the advantage of less ballast
would be obtained.

"The benefits accruing to the plan here outlined were observed and appreciated on several occasions when the boat was
given her preliminary trials.   During these trials the ballasting
by means of the tanks was manipulated in such a perfect manner that her performances astounded yachting men.   To use nau-
tical terms, she was stiff as a church in heavy weather and like
a witch in a light wind.   Her performances in heavy weather
were especially noted, and she soon came be known as a boat
of great stability.

"Let us now return to the time immediately preceding the

first race for the International Trophy. Both boats were officially measured the day before the date set for the first race.
The American boat, naturally, was as light as she could be
made. In other words, her tanks were empty when the measurement was taken. During the afternoon of that day there
was a strong breeze blowing. The weather was threatening,
and there was every indication that the next day, the day of the
race, would be a stormy one.

"There was only one other man on the boat, in addition to
its ostensible owner, who understood the manipulation of the
tanks. A conference was held between them, and it was decided that if the then present condition of the weather continued
during the night, the tanks were to be filled. The owner left
the boat early in the evening.

"The threatening weather lasted until far into the night,
and in anticipation of its continuance the following day, the
tanks were filled and the eleven tons of ballast added.

"It is here that the mistake, referred to in the opening of
this address and which led to the controversy, occurred. But
it was made by the man who had charge of the tanks on the
American boat, not by the English owner.

"Contrary to what had been anticipated, a change in the
weather took place toward sunrise of the day of the race. The
wind died out until there was hardly a fair sailing breeze left.
Before this discovery was made by the man who had filled the
tanks, and while the boat, lying in comparatively still water,
had the extra ballast in her, persons on board the English yacht
noticed her condition. They readily discerned that she was
more deeply immersed than she was when they last saw her.

"The attention of the English owner was called to the ap-

parent fact, and—but the remainder of that part of the story
has been told before.

"Now, may it please the honorable court, it is contended
that if the English owner's request that the yacht should be
remeasured that night had been granted, the result would not
have been materially changed. She would have shown the
same load water line as when previously measured.

"This can be easily explained. When the American owner
boarded his boat that morning and realized the unfortunate condition of affairs resulting from his trusted employee's failure to prog-
nosticate the true state of the weather, there is no official record
showing that he gave utterance to the emotions which undoubt-
edly arose within him, but it is quite reasonable to suppose, that,
like a famous historical personage, 'he did a heap of thinking.'

"It was too late then to remedy the mistake that had been
made, but as soon as the boat was under way out in the open
sea, the pump was set at work and the tanks emptied as rapidly
as possible. They were completely emptied before the race was
half finished, and the American boat crossed the line a winner
sailing on the same water line as when she was first measured.

"The only opportunity that the English owner had of
proving the correctness of his assertion, was to have refused to
sail the race until the boats had been remeasured.

"And now, having thus with more detail than was perhaps
necessary, recounted the conclusions reached from the evidence
we have secured, I shall proceed to present said evidence in
regular order. The first offered is a drawing of the American
boat marked exhibit 'A.' It gives a side view of the vessel,
showing the location of the tanks and steward's quarters, and
the arrangement of the braces in the lower hold:

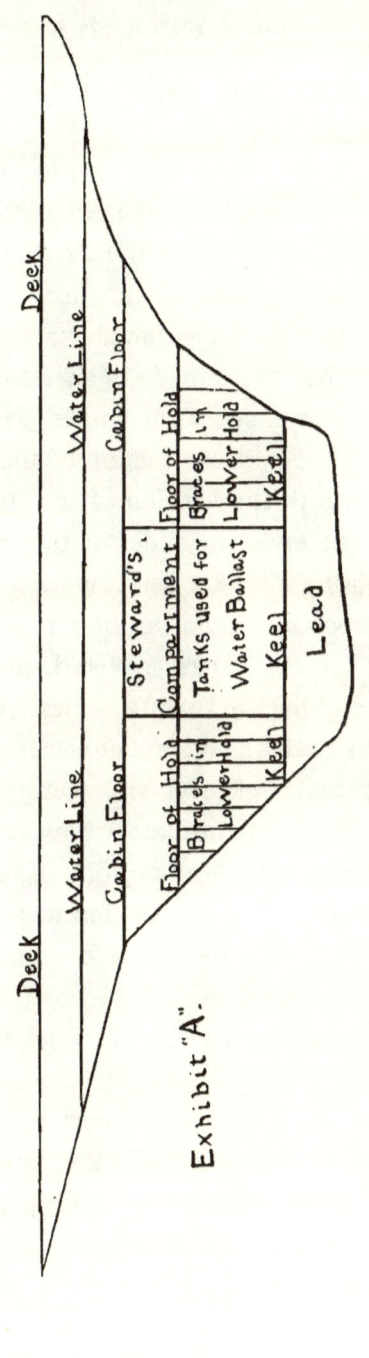

Exhibit "A".

Deck

Water Line

Cabin Floor

Floor of Hold

Steward's Compartment

Tanks used for Water Ballast

Keel

Lead

Floor of Hold

Braces in Lower Hold

Keel

Braces in Lower Hold

Keel

" May it please the court, I will now offer several affidavits. The first is that of John Doe, Sr.

" ' I, John Doe, Sr., being duly sworn, do depose and say: I was employed by the builder of the American yacht, as superintendent of construction. After the boat had been launched and taken away to her permanent anchorage, I was instructed to build two tanks for her. The tanks were taken on board the boat in sections. They were made of sheets of steel.

" ' With the assistance of one other person, I placed the tanks in position in the midship section of the lower hold of the boat directly underneath the flooring of the steward's section of the upper hold. The ends and sides of the tanks reached from the keel to the flooring above. They were securely fastened to the frames of the boat and could not be removed.

" ' The sides of the tanks covered seven frames. The frames were from eighteen to twenty inches apart. When completed, these tanks, which were connected by pipes, had a capacity of about 385 cubic feet and were capable of holding 2,880 gallons of water. I do not know how the tanks were connected on the outside. After my work of putting the tanks together and fastening them in position had been completed, I was not again allowed to go below deck. I have not, since that time, been below the cabin deck of the boat.'

" The next is from the person who assisted in putting the tanks in position.

" ' I, John Doe, Jr., being duly sworn, do depose and say: I was employed by the firm that built the American boat as assistant superintendent of construction. I supervised the making of the plates for the tanks ordered for the boat after she had been launched and taken away from the yards. The plates were taken on board the boat at different times and stowed below.

"'When all the plates had arrived, I assisted another person in putting them together and making the tanks. The tanks were built in the midship section, underneath the cook's galley, and reached from the keel to the floor of the upper hold. They were connected by means of pipes. I have no knowledge as to the manner in which they were connected with pipes on the outside. After the work of putting the tanks in place had been finished I was not again allowed below decks. I have seen the boat only once since that time.

"'By their measurement I know that the tanks had a capacity of 385 cubic feet, and would hold, when full, about 23,870 pounds of water. I did not know what the tanks were to be used for. Nothing had ever been said about their use, and I had become too wise to ask questions.'

"The next offered is that of the man who connected the tanks with the pipes on the outside leading to the pump and intake hole:

"'I, George Gordon, being duly sworn, do depose and say: I am a plumber, doing business on my own account. One day during the spring of 1695, a gentleman called at my place of business and told me that he wanted me to do a little job. I asked him what it was. He told me it was to make some pipe connections on board a boat. I said I would send one of my men. He said no, that wouldn't do at all. He said that I must go and do the job myself. He promised big money for it. He said that he had been recommended to me as a man who could be trusted. He said there was nothing wrong about the job, but that he didn't want anybody to know anything about it. I asked him where the boat was. He said she was a great distance away.

" 'I took what tools I thought I might need and went with him to the boat. She was a yacht, and I have since learned that she was the boat that beat the Englishman. I went down in the lower hold and there found, in the center of the boat, what looked at first like a big tank. I found out after that there were two tanks, placed close together. The man showed me two pipes, the ends of which were close to the bottom of the tank on one side of the boat. He told me that he wanted those pipes connected with the tank.

" 'It was a hard job on account of the small amount of room I had to work in. But I made the connections all right. The man then took me on an upper deck and took me into a small room or closet like. It looked like a water closet. In there was a large brass pump, unlike anything I had ever seen before. I began to examine the pump. I was curious to know what it was. The man told me to never mind the pump, but go on with my work. He said that he wanted a pipe that came up near the pump connected with it. I asked him where the other pipe was, and he told me it was none of my business. All I had to do was to connect that one pipe with the pump. I did that soon enough, got my money, picked up my tools and went home.

" 'As I was going away the man told me not to mention the job I had done to anyone. I have never seen the boat since.'

" The next deposition is from the man whose mistake on the night preceding the day of the race caused all the trouble:

" 'I, Richard Roe, being duly sworn do depose and say: I was employed on the American boat from the day she was launched until she was permanently laid up after the races. I was known as one of the crew, but my name did not appear on the books of the boat in any capacity. I was under orders only to the owner of the boat and was responsible only to him.

" 'It was my duty to take care of the water tanks that were located amidships, to let in the water when it was needed, and to set the pump working when they wanted the water out. The pump was a curious affair, and I never knew exactly how it worked. The man who put the pump in showed me how to set it going and how to stop it, and that's all I ever knew about it.

" 'The pump was situated in a water closet on the starboard side. The mouth of the pipe that let the water into the tanks was also there. When the weather was heavy and we needed more ballast, all I had to do was to pull up the cut-off at the mouth of the pipe and the water would rush into the tanks. The mouth of the pipe was situated below the water line and was always covered, even when the boat had no ballast in her. If, as happened several times during the trials, the wind died out and we wanted to lighten the boat, all I had to do was to push down the cut-off and start the pump working. The water would escape through the water closet hole, which was always under water, except when the boat was tacking and was heeled over on the port side. When this happened, I would stop the pump and wait until the boat turned on a tack and heeled over to the starboard side. Then I would set the pump working again. I was told to be careful about this, for if any one should see the water coming out of the pipe hole while the boat was heeled over on the port side, it might give the whole snap away.

" 'There was only one man, to my knowledge on the boat besides myself, who understood how to work the pump and pipe. That was the man from whom I took my orders and to whom I was responsible. I am positive that not one of the crew knew anything about it.

" ' On the evening before the first race with the Englishman, my employer called me aside and told me that he thought we were going to have a stormy day for the race. He said that if the weather continued as threatening as it then was during the night—that is, if it did not appear to be dying out and that it would be stormy the next day—I was to fill the tanks, as the boat would need the extra ballast to carry all her sails.

" ' He left early that evening, after telling me again to watch the weather carefully. I did watch it carefully. Along toward 11 o'clock that night it was very threatening and it looked certain we would have a stormy day. Before I turned in I pulled up the cut-off and let the water run into the tanks. I then turned in and slept till day-break the next morning. When I got up on deck, I found that the wind had died out almost entirely, and that every thing indicated a clear day with little wind.

" ' I didn't know what to do about it. I knew that the water shouldn't be in those tanks in that kind of weather, but I was under strict orders never to touch the pump or cut-off unless I was told to do so by my employer. When he arrived a few hours later he saw at once the fix I had got myself into. He blamed me for turning on the water so soon. He said I should have waited until I was sure about the weather.

" ' I told him I thought I was sure, that the change happened after I had turned in. I suppose I should have waited until morning before turning on the water, but I was tired and wanted to turn in and I took a chance.

" ' I asked him what I should do about it. He told me to wait. Soon after the boats had started on the race, he told me to start the pump. I did so, and before we were on the return to the finish the water was all out of the tanks. We didn't use the tanks again. The next day they put marks on the side of the boat and I never got word to let the water in again. In fact I was never allowed in the water closet again. My employer took my key away from me and kept it.

" 'I don't know how much water the tanks held, but it must have been a great deal. It took some time to fill them and a longer time to pump them out. I knew it must have been a great deal, for the boat was as stiff as a house when they were full. You could blow her stick out of her before she would show her keel.'

" And now, may it please the court, we will close the argument. We have sought a rehearing of the case because we are convinced, in the light of recent developments, that a serious error had been committed. The evidence that we have submitted is sufficient, in our opinion, to raise a question of reasonable doubt, on which this action is based.

"I have submitted a brief in which are recounted the essential points brought out at the first investigation. We will now leave it to the honorable court to decide

"WHICH WAS RIGHT?"